GHOSTS AND GHOULS

The Grimwort Ghosts

The Grimworts were different from other families. They liked dark dungeons and slimy cellars, where no light ever reached. They liked cobwebs and spiders and things that go bump in the night, because the Grimworts weren't ordinary people, they were ghosts.

In an ancient tower, in the middle of a very old city, the Grimworts happily haunted the draughty stairwells and creepy corridors. They loved nothing more than to scare the socks off any visitors who came to call. They especially liked scaring children, because they seemed to scream longer and louder than adults. In fact, the louder the children screamed, the funnier the Grimworts found it. All day long, they lurked silently in the shadows, waiting for visitors to pass by.

However, the mischievous ghost family had a problem. Egor, the youngest ghost wasn't very good at scaring people. He just couldn't get the hang of it. His parents were very worried. "Do a blood-curdling scream," said Lord Grimwort, one day. So, Egor opened his mouth, as wide as he could, but for some reason, the tiniest, squeakiest, "Oooooooh," sound came out.

Lord and Lady Grimwort looked at each other very worriedly.
"Really, Egor," said his mother, "what is the point of being a ghost if you can't scare people?"

Lord Grimwort stood up. "A really good, blood-curdling scream sounds like this," he said, opening his mouth so wide, you could see what he'd eaten for breakfast three hundred years ago, when he was still alive.
"AAAARGH!" he screamed. The rats in the dungeon ran for cover and the bats dropped from the ceiling. Egor put his fingers in his ears. His father's screams were really deafening.

The Grimwort Ghosts

"I can rattle my chains," said Egor, "they're scary." He gave his chains a good shake, but they just sounded like a baby shaking a rattle.
"Oh, dear," said Lady Grimwort, disappearing through the dungeon wall. "What are we going to do with you, Egor?"

Lord Grimwort looked at the clock. "Some children are coming to visit the dungeons this afternoon. Let's give them a big fright." he said, with a dastardly cackle.

Everyone got ready for the haunting. Egor's brother, Oswald, slipped into his costume with bloodstains down the front. "I like scaring children," he cackled. Edmund put on a black hood with slits for eyes. He picked up an axe, swung it high in the air and waved it around.
"Come on," said Lord Grimwort, "it's time to take our places."

The Grimwort Ghosts

Lady Grimwort put on her 'lady about to be beheaded' costume, practiced one of her spine-chilling wails and the whole family moved off in the direction of the dungeons.

The dungeons were dark and dank, and eerie shadows slunk in corners. Lord Grimwort suddenly pointed at a rotting, old, empty barrel. "This is what I want you to do, Egor," he said. "I want you to hide in this big wooden barrel and when the children come in, I want you to pop your head up and give them a fright."

Egor's father lifted him into the barrel. "Where will you be?" Egor asked. "We're going to scare the tour guides further down the passage," said Lord Grimwort with a happy smile.
Lady Grimwort kissed Egor. "Be my spookiest son, darling," she said.

The Grimwort Ghosts

Egor settled down and waited. It was comfy in the barrel, but a little too warm for Egor. He liked things nice and chilly. After a few minutes, Egor's eyes started to close. He was almost asleep when he heard noises. "Ugh, this is horrid," said a girl's voice.

"It's creepy," said another voice. "Imagine being imprisoned down here."

"What are those rings on the wall for?" asked a boy with glasses.

"Prisoners were chained there, long ago, and then left to rot," said the teacher. The children looked around. The dungeon was sinister and they didn't like the way it made shivers run down their spines.

Inside the barrel, Egor stood up behind the classmates. He blew his cold, ghostly breath over them. The children felt the hairs standing up on their arms and the backs of their necks, but they didn't know why.

Egor slunk down into the barrel and then jumped up, suddenly. "Whoo!" he wailed and ducked down again. Everyone turned to look.
"Was that you, Adrian?" asked the teacher, looking at a boy with spiky hair.
"No, Miss Jones," said Adrian, glancing nervously around.

Egor rose up again. "Whoo!" he moaned, right in front of the children. Their mouths fell open and their eyes nearly popped out of their heads. Adrian's spiky hair stood up so high, he looked like a hedgehog. The children all screamed at once.

Egor was so surprised, he fell back inside the barrel and banged his chin. "Oooh," he cried, with a long, mournful moan, "Ooooooh!"
The sound echoed in the barrel and seemed to move all around the dark, dank dungeon.

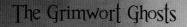

The children were rigid with fright. Then suddenly, they started screaming again and made a mad dash for the door. "Wait," called the teacher, nervously, beginning to run after them. They didn't stop running until they were outside in the warm sunshine.

Egor's family listened with glee from further down the passage. "What terrifying screams," said Lord Grimwort, "how marvellous!"

The Grimwort Ghosts

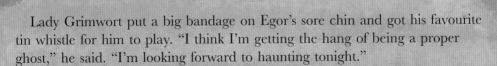

Lady Grimwort put a big bandage on Egor's sore chin and got his favourite tin whistle for him to play. "I think I'm getting the hang of being a proper ghost," he said. "I'm looking forward to haunting tonight."

After that, visitors to the old tower were more scared than ever. They said that they felt cold breaths of air that sent shivers down their spines and heard eerie noises coming from the dungeons. Little did they know that, at last, Egor had become a very scary Grimwort ghost.

The Ghost Ship

Lawrence stood on the deck of the old pirate ship. It had long since left the sea and been moored in the middle of a busy theme park. His class was on a day trip and it should have been the best fun ever. The trouble was, it was turning out to be no fun at all. Ryan Twigg was trying to bully Lawrence into ringing a big bell that stood on the main deck of the great ship.

Lawrence saw the sign above the bell and it made him nervous. "Genuine bell from the real pirate ship, *The Revenge*. DO NOT RING, or you will summon the pirate ghosts," he read out loud.

"Come on, Lawrence," interrupted Ryan, "you don't want everyone to think you're a coward, do you?" There were muffled chuckles and giggles from the other children, but Lawrence didn't find it funny. What if the bell really did summon the pirate ghosts?

Suddenly, Ryan reached out and tugged at the big bell. "Run, everyone!" he cried, as he raced off, leaving Lawrence standing on the deck, holding his hands over his ears to dull the deafening sound.

The ringing stopped abruptly. Everything went quiet and a heavy silence fell. Then, Lawrence noticed that something very strange was happening.

The Ghost Ship

The deck of the ship began to shake and strange forms rose out of the wooden floor. Ragged-looking skeleton sailors appeared, wearing old-fashioned clothes. They surrounded Lawrence, their dry bones clattering as they moved.

The tallest of the pirate ghosts stepped forward. He had a skull face, rimmed with a huge, red beard. "I am Captain Redbeard of the pirate ship, *The Revenge*," he announced.

The captain swept off his wide-brimmed hat and bowed to Lawrence. "We have been cursed by a powerful sea-witch, to only rise up when the ship's bell rings. We are doomed to live inside this fairground and never see the sea again. That is, unless we can unlock our treasure chest." Just then, a ghostly chest rose up from the floor, locked with a gigantic padlock.

The Ghost Ship

Lawrence should have been scared, but he wasn't. The sea-witch's curse seemed very unfair. "Where's the key to the lock?" he asked.
"It is out of our reach, forever," replied the captain, sadly. "It lies in the ship's hull and is guarded by a deadly, giant octopus. Only someone who does not dwell in the land of ghosts can lift the curse."

Lawrence felt sorry for the ghost pirates. "Perhaps I could fetch the key for you?" he said.
The captain was very surprised. "You're braver than you look," he said.

The Ghost Ship

Without another word, Lawrence strode over to the cabin door at the side of the ship and stepped down into the eerie gloom of the dark, wet hold below.

The rickety wooden steps were old and slimy. As he stepped down them, Lawrence saw the ghostly octopus. It had huge eyes with slit pupils and a razor-sharp beak. Its eight tentacles writhed and squirmed, dripping thick slime all over the floor. In one of its tentacles was a shiny, golden key.

The Ghost Ship

Lawrence shook with fear and stepped down again, but the rotting wood gave way and he slipped. The huge, squelching body of the octopus moved closer. It's eyes grew black with anger. It raised its huge tentacles, splattering slime everywhere and tried to grab Lawrence.

Panicking and gasping for breath, Lawrence tried in vain to grab the key. He struggled, slipping on the stinking slime until the spectral octopus loomed over him, snapping its lethal beak. Lawrence thrashed and kicked with all his strength, then suddenly, he touched something hard and cold. He had managed to grab the key.

The octopus let out an unearthly scream and began to disappear. Shaking, Lawrence scrambled back up the steps as fast as his trembling legs could carry him.

The Ghost Ship

Back on deck, Captain Redbeard unlocked the chest. Inside, piles of ghostly treasure glittered and gleamed. "We're free of the curse!" cried the captain, and all of the pirates cheered. Captain Redbeard turned to Lawrence. "You saved us all, young lad. What can we do for you before we return to the sea?"

Lawrence couldn't think of anything at first. Then he saw Ryan and his friends come on board. They had come back to see if Lawrence had got into trouble for ringing the bell. Lawrence quickly whispered something to the captain, who suddenly disappeared with his crew.

"Did you go crying to the teacher?" taunted Ryan.

The Ghost Ship

Suddenly, the mist rose up from the deck. Captain Redbeard appeared, waving a huge, pirate cutlass. "Shiver me timbers!" he bellowed. "Show me the scurvy dog who does bully brave shipmate, Lawrence, and I'll run him through."

Ryan looked up in horror at the fierce pirate and his terrible sword. His lower lip quivered, as if he was about to cry, then he ran screaming from the deck, followed by his friends. Captain Redbeard chuckled, winked at Lawrence and disappeared.

After that, no one ever bullied Lawrence again and it was all thanks to a ringing bell on a cursed ghost ship.

The Phantom

Mr Pratchett was getting impatient. "Hurry up, boys," he shouted. "The light's fading and we don't want to set up camp in the dark." It was Summerhill High's annual trip to the wilderness and things weren't going well. The school bus driver had already fixed a flat tyre and now they were lost.

There was a lot of noisy laughter from the group of boys on the bus. Joe, Billy and Alex looked out of the back window. Miss Meeks, their teacher, was asking a bewildered, red-faced man for directions. The man was pointing somewhere in the distance and looked concerned.

The bus juddered into life. Miss Meeks jumped on board and slumped into the seat next to Mr Pratchett. "Honestly," she said, "all I wanted were directions to the campsite. That man went on and on about some figure that roams the moors, a phantom or something. I've never heard anything so ridiculous. Anyway, there's a left hand turn somewhere up the road. It's easy to miss, so we'll have to be careful."

The bus pulled off with a slow rumble. Billy and Joe had heard Miss Meeks talking. "A phantom on the moor," said Billy, "this could be an interesting trip." The boys looked out of the back window. The red-faced man stood with his arms crossed, shaking his head. The sun was sinking and a faint veil of mist had slunk slowly down the mountainside.

The Phantom

It was dark by the time Mr Pratchett realised that they were lost again. The boys tried to stifle their laughter. They loved it when teachers messed up. "We'll have to camp on the moor tonight," said Mr Pratchett, with a sigh. "Come on, you lot, follow me."

Billy, Joe and Alex grabbed their stuff and joined the line of boys following the teacher's torchlight. After a while, Alex hung back, "I think I've dropped my compass," he said, "I won't be a minute." Miss Meeks told him to hurry up.

The Phantom

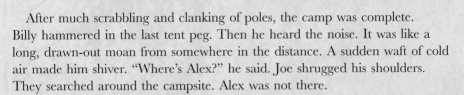

After much scrabbling and clanking of poles, the camp was complete.
Billy hammered in the last tent peg. Then he heard the noise. It was like a
long, drawn-out moan from somewhere in the distance. A sudden waft of cold
air made him shiver. "Where's Alex?" he said. Joe shrugged his shoulders.
They searched around the campsite. Alex was not there.

It fell to Mr Pratchett to search for the missing boy. He set off into the dark,
calling Alex's name. Billy thought he saw a shaft of light moving nearby.
He called out, but no-one answered. "It must be the wind," he said to Joe.

The boys climbed into their tents and zipped up the flapping canvas. In the
distance, they could hear Mr Pratchett calling out. Billy felt uneasy.
Suddenly there was a loud cry on the moor.

Everyone scrambled out of their tents. "What was that?" said a scared voice. Miss Meeks pushed into the group of boys holding torches. "Quiet boys," she said, "I'm going to look for Alex and Mr Pratchett. Stay here and don't move."

Miss Meeks set off, alone, into the black night and most of the boys went back to bed. Billy and Joe remained, feeling anxious.

The wind curled and snaked around the camp, rattling pans and rustling canvas. A strange moaning echoed and Billy was sure he saw the silhouette of a woman watching them. "Is that you, Miss Meeks?" he said. But no one answered.

The Phantom

Suddenly, a terrible scream came from the moor. There was a flurry of
movement as the other boys scrambled out of their tents.
"This is creepy," said one nervous boy.
"Ssssh," said Joe, "let's listen."
A hulking figure was moving in the darkness. From its centre, a small light
winked on and off, like a glittering eye. It squelched and groaned, then it let out
a series of short gasps and grunts. "It's the phantom," stuttered Billy, "it's real."

The Phantom

Each boy shone a torch towards the thing on the moor. It had three sets of eyes and it was the ugliest thing they had ever seen. They stared as it lurched closer and closer, until the creature was nearly in the camp.

Suddenly, the beast spoke, "Stop shining that light in my eyes!" It was Mr Pratchett and he wasn't happy. In fact, he was in a foul mood. He hobbled into the camp, covered from head to toe in mud. Clinging to him were Miss Meeks and Alex.